16 NOV 2017
- 9 JUL 2018
0 3 SEP 2021

Please return this book on or before the date shown above. To renew go to www.essex.gov.uk/libraries, ring 0345 603 7628 or go to any Essex library.

Essex County Council

ORCHARD BOOKS
Carmelite House, 50 Victoria Embankment, London EC4Y 0DZ
Orchard Books Australia
Level 17/207 Kent Street, Sydney, NSW 2000

First published in 1998 under the title
BEN THE BENDIEST BOY by Orchard Books
This updated version published in 2015

ISBN: 978 1 40833 758 5

Text © Laurence Anholt 2015
Illustrations © Tony Ross 1998

A CIP catalogue record for this book is available
from the British Library.

1 3 5 7 9 10 8 6 4 2

Printed and bound by CPI Group (UK) Ltd, Croydon CR0 4YY

MIX
Paper from
responsible sources
FSC® C104740
www.fsc.org

The paper and board used in this book are made from wood
from responsible sources.

Orchard Books is an imprint of Hachette Children's Group and published by
the Watts Publishing Group Limited, an Hachette UK company.

www.hachette.co.uk

Bendy
BEN

Laurence Anholt

Illustrated by Tony Ross

ORCHARD

www.anholt.co.uk

Hee, hee, hello everyone!
My name is **Ruby** and I have the
funniest family in the world.
In these books, I will introduce you
to my **freaky family**.

You will meet people like…

But this book is all about…my cousin **BENDY BEN**!

We are going to meet my cousin
Ben, the bendiest boy ever born.
Nobody is bendier than Ben.

My cousin Ben is as bendy as a banana.

My cousin Ben is as bendy as an elastic band.

My cousin Ben is as bendy as spaghetti.

My cousin Ben is as bendy as a garden hose.

If you don't believe how bendy Ben is, just watch him blow his nose.

As well as being bendy, Ben is a boy scout. He is the bendiest boy scout there has ever been.

It can be useful to be bendy when you are a boy scout. You can win all the best boy-scout badges.

Ben wins the 'Best Boy-Scout
Boomerang Badge'.

Ben wins the 'Bounciest Boy-Scout Trampoline Badge'.

Ben wins nearly every boy-scout
badge you can think of.
Ben only needs
one more boy-scout
badge to win the
biggest boy-scout
prize of all.

Then my cousin Ben will be the
BEST BOY SCOUT THERE HAS
EVER BEEN!

The big Boy Scout Leader says,
"Ben, you should try to win
the 'Best Boy-Scout Marching
Badge'."

But Ben is too bendy to march.

The big Boy Scout Leader says,
"Ben, you should try to win the
'Sit Silent And Still On A Stool All
Saturday Badge'."

But Ben is too bored and bendy
to sit silent and still on a stool all
Saturday.

Then the big Boy Scout Leader has an idea.

He says, "Ben, there is one badge you will be sure to win…the 'Boogie-Woogie Groovy Bendy Boy-Scout Break Dance Badge'."

"Oh boy!" says Ben. "I would love to try."

So when the boogie-woogie music
begins, Ben begins to dance.

He dances the 'Humpy Lumpy
Camel Dance'.

Everybody claps.

He dances the 'Jelly Belly Jumping Jive Dance'.

Everybody claps and cheers.

He dances the 'Roly Poly Football Goalie Bounce It On Your Head Dance'.

Everybody claps and cheers and
whistles.

Then, last of all, Ben dances the 'Clippy Clappy Snippy Snappy Swirly Whirly Snake Dance'.

It is the best bendy dance the boy
scouts and the big Boy Scout
Leader have ever seen.

It is the bendiest, trendiest boy-scout
dance there has ever been.

Ben bends downwards.

Ben bends upwards.

Ben bends forwards.

Ben bends backwards.

But then...

Ben's knees get stuck round his
ears.

Ben's toes get stuck in his nose.

Ben's elbows get stuck round his knees.

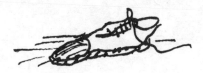

And his fingers get tied into bows.

"Oh boy!" says my cousin Ben.
"I seem to be sort of stuck."

"Oh boy!" say all the boy scouts.
"What bad luck."

"Will I win the 'Boogie-Woogie Groovy Bendy Boy-Scout Break Dance Badge'?" asks Ben.
"No," says the big Boy Scout Leader. "You will not. Because you are tied in a knot."

My cousin Ben bends his head sadly.

"BUT," says the big Boy Scout
Leader, "you will win the 'Top
Boy-Scout Knot Badge'!"

"OH BOY!" shouts Ben. "Now I have ALL the best boy-scout badges. Now I am the Best Bendy Boy Scout in the world."

And when the other boy scouts
untie Ben, they each win a
'Top Untying Knot Badge'.

"OH BOY!" bellow all the boy
scouts. "Bravo Ben!"

Then the boy scouts clap and cheer
and whistle.

And my cousin Ben bows a big bendy bow and beams the biggest, bendiest smile that any boy scout has ever seen.

THE END

My
FREAKY
FAMILY

COLLECT THEM ALL!

Also available as an ebook